My wonderful friend - Celia

for your Birthday!

July 5th 1999

A South-African Classic truly told.

JOCK OF THE BUSHVELD

Sir Percy Fitzpatrick's classic as retold by
PHILLIDA BROOKE SIMONS

Illustrations by
ANGUS McBRIDE

D1638985

Contents

Thinking of you with Love Amelia

STRUIK TIMMINS

Into the Bushveld

In 1884, before the great city of Johannesburg existed and when herds of wild animals still roamed the empty veld, a young man named Percy Fitzpatrick left his home at the Cape to seek adventure in the Eastern Transvaal. Gold had been discovered near Lydenburg a few years before and people had flocked there to dig with pick and shovel in the hopes of finding a fortune. A few were lucky and returned home rich men, but most of them discovered nothing but disappointment.

Among these unsuccessful diggers was Percy Fitzpatrick, but he refused to be discouraged. He might not have found gold, he told himself, but at least he could experience adventure. So he bought a wagon and a team of oxen and earned his living by carrying stores of food and other necessities from Delagoa Bay to the goldfields, some 400 kilometres inland.

It was a hard life, for between the high plains of the Transvaal and the sea lay the wilderness of the Bushveld. Roads were no more than rough tracks. The wagons that rumbled along them were cumbersome and the oxen slow. And always, to man and animal, there was the danger of fever. By day the sun blazed down on rolling grasslands dotted with twisted thorn trees. By night the rocky hills echoed with the eerie call of jackal and hyena and with the threatening roar of the lion.

No man would dream of travelling in the Bushveld without his gun. He might need it for self-defence, to shoot a striking cobra or a springing leopard. But he would need it also to kill 'for the pot'. Food was scarce and to obtain it he must bring down the graceful impala or the stately kudu, beautiful and harmless though these creatures might be.

It was, besides, a lonely life out there on the veld. If a man was lucky he might have a dog to take hunting and to be his companion at the camp fire on a clear winter night. And Percy Fitzpatrick was fortunate to have a very special dog, a clever and loyal dog whose courage knew no bounds – Jock, the hero of these tales.

Many years after he had left the Bushveld, Percy Fitzpatrick told Jock's adventures as bedtime stories to his three children. By then he was a successful businessman and well-known politician in Johannesburg and the children, encouraged by their friend Rudyard Kipling, begged their father to write the stories down for other children to enjoy.

So, in 1907, *Jock of the Bushveld* was first published. Before long it had become one of the most beloved of all dog stories and today it ranks proudly among the greatest of South African classics.

Transport riding

Before the days of railways or motor trucks, goods were carried from the seaports of southern Africa to the inland towns and villages by heavy covered wagons, often travelling in convoy. Each wagon was drawn by a team of 12 to 16 oxen and the men who owned them were known as transport riders.

Because it was often very hot during the day, the wagons travelled in two four-hour shifts. The first was before sunrise and the second after sunset. Roads were bad and the oxen moved slowly, so the wagons seldom covered more than 30 kilometres in a day. At the end of each shift, or trek, the wagons were outspanned in a sheltered spot where the men rested in camp until it was time for the next trek to begin. They then inspanned the oxen and set off again.

Jess

No one could have called Jess beautiful.

She was a bull terrier with a dull brindled coat marked with shadowy grey and black stripes. Her eyes were small and cross-looking and she had restless, twitching ears. She was bad-tempered, too, and most unsociable. But to her master she was as brave and faithful a dog as ever lived.

Jess was the only dog at our camp. She belonged to my friend, Ted, and she never left his side, day or night. He was lucky to have her, for good dogs were difficult to find on the goldfields. I tried to get one for myself before I joined the wagons going down to Delagoa Bay but I had no success. I wanted a dog to be my companion and to go out hunting with me, for game was still plentiful then and we always needed meat for our camp cooking-pot. Every day the other men brought back something they had shot. It might be a duiker or reedbuck or a wild pig, but I always seemed to return empty-handed.

Yes, what I wanted was a good hunting dog. I needed a dog with sense and strength and plenty of courage – a dog like Jess. She was certainly not a favourite among us but we could not help respecting her, especially after that day at Ship Mountain.

Ship Mountain was a pleasant place on the Bushveld where we had rested during the heat of the day. At sundown, just as we were preparing to leave on our evening trek, some wagons passed by. Ted knew the owner so he decided to go ahead with them, planning to meet us at the next outspan. He called to Jess as he jumped onto the wagon. Immediately she ran out to him from a patch of long grass where she had been lying. But when she saw Ted moving off with the other wagons she did not follow him. Instead, she sat down in the middle of the road, looking after her master with an anxious, puzzled expression.

The wagons disappeared and Jess went back to her grass patch. A moment later she returned, whimpering softly and obviously worried. She ran restlessly to and fro between the long grass and the road all the time we were inspanning. It seemed that she could not make up her mind whether to follow or to stay.

The last and most important things to be loaded onto the wagons were our guns and water barrel. They had been left close to the place where Jess was lying and when we were almost ready to leave, one of the Zulu wagon drivers went to collect them. Within a few moments he returned to us at the wagons in a state of great excitement. 'Ow!' he exclaimed. 'That dog Jess! I think she's mad! Every time I go near the guns she tries to bite me!' And he refused to go back.

There was nothing for it but to collect the guns and water barrel ourselves. We walked towards the grass patch and when we were a short way off Jess appeared. She was crouching low as if she were about to spring at us. Her ears were laid back flat, her teeth were bared and, as we watched, the hair along her back slowly began to bristle. There was no doubt about it, Jess did not want any of us near her.

We tried coaxing her but that was no use. Then we scolded her and that was no good either, but somehow we had to get hold of our guns. We were almost at our wits' end, wondering what to do next, when we heard a faint but unmistakable sound. We stood silent, listening. And then from the grass where Jess had been lying there came softly but clearly the cry of a very young puppy. Now we knew the reason for Jess's strange behaviour!

We sent for Ted at once. When he arrived at our wagons a couple of hours later Jess ran out to greet him. She jumped up at his chest with a long, trembling whimper of welcome. Then she darted straight ahead of him to her nest in the grass. Ted took a lantern and went to look at the puppies but Jess stood over them so that he could not get too close. We knew that she would never bite her master, but when he tried to pick up one of the puppies it was too much for her. She gave a low cry, caught his wrist in her mouth and gently but firmly held it.

That was Jess – and Jess was the mother of Jock.

The pick of the puppies

There were six puppies and in one of the wagons we made a roomy nest for them. We had their tails cut short but found out afterwards that we had made a mistake. Bull terriers should always have short ears and long tails. Five of the puppies were fat, strong, yellow little chaps. They were just like their father, so Ted said, and he was the best of his breed in the Transvaal. Only the sixth puppy was at all like Jess, and he was an ugly, miserable little creature. He was not yellow like the others, nor was he brindled like his mother. He was a dirty, pale colour with faint wavy lines in his coat and a sharp, wizened little muzzle.

The men on our wagons called him 'the rat'. They said he spoilt the litter and should be drowned. But to me, any dog seemed better than none, so I offered to take him myself. Naturally, I would have preferred one of the big puppies, but Ted had promised them all to his friends long before.

Poor little rat! I could not help feeling sorry for him. The other puppies trampled on him and bullied him horribly. They pushed him away from his food so that he hurriedly gobbled up whatever scraps he could find. As a result his tummy swelled like a little balloon. He had bandy legs and his thin neck made his large head seem even bigger than it was. His ears were lopsided and the really silly thing was that the little fellow did not realize how ugly he was. Far from it! He strutted about in the camp as if he owned the whole wide world.

As the puppies grew older I began to notice things about the odd one. No matter how many of the puppies packed on top of him, how they bit or mauled him, he never let out a yelp. He would lie on his back, snapping to left and right. He would grab a leg or an ear and hang on with his needle-sharp teeth until the other puppy cleared off, nursing an injured paw or holding his head on one side. I used to praise him for his courage but the other men only laughed at me. They said I was trying to make the best of a bad job so I gave up talking about him altogether.

At last the puppies were ready to go to their new owners. I was still hoping that someone might change his mind and I would get one of the big ones after all, but there seemed little chance of that. So one afternoon when Ted suddenly announced: 'Billy Griffiths can't take his pup!' we were all astonished. Billy's was first pick, the champion of the litter. Straight away several of the others offered to exchange their puppies for his, but Ted only shook his head. 'No', he said. 'You had a good pick in the beginning.' And he turned to me: 'You've only had the leftover,' he smiled. 'You can have Billy's pup!'

It seemed too good to be true! I barely thanked Ted before rushing off to look at my pup. I lifted him up and examined him closely. He was a fine strong fellow with a dark muzzle and a gleaming yellow coat. I certainly would be proud to own him.

I put him down and turned to go but just then the odd puppy waddled up to me in the friendliest manner. Poor little chap! In my excitement I had forgotten all about him. I walked back to the others and suddenly there was a shout of laughter. 'The rat' was trotting along behind me, head erect, ears cocked and his stumpy tail twiddling away. He seemed to think that I was his master and that he should follow me wherever I went.

That night I fell asleep thinking of the two of them, the best and the worst in the litter. But when I woke next morning, it was the odd puppy that I had on my mind. How would he feel when he found that he was to be left behind or given to anyone willing to take him? Would he think that he had been deserted?

In the morning, while walking beside the wagons in the early trek, I thought of all the wretched puppies I had heard of that grew into wonderful dogs, and of all the great and famous men who had once been very ordinary children.

By breakfast time my mind was made up. 'Ted,' I said as we met round the fire with our steaming mugs of coffee, 'I won't be taking Billy's pup after all. I think I'll stick to "the rat".'

An astonished silence followed. Then there was a chorus of 'Well, I'll be hanged!' But I had made my choice. And from that day on I had as my friend and companion the best and bravest dog in all the world.

Jock's schooldays

Once I had made my choice no one ever again spoke of 'the rat' or 'the odd puppy'. The men at our camp soon stopped laughing at him. They began to respect him so that when he was given a name they respected that too.

And his name was Jock.

He had begun life by being small and weak. He had been bullied so badly by the other puppies that he soon learnt that if he wanted something he had to fight for it. One day he fought two of the big puppies, one after the other, for his bone and beat them both off. We all saw the tussle and cheered the plucky little chap. After that, the moment a puppy saw Jock walking slowly and carefully towards him he seemed to get tired of his bone and walked away. And so the other dogs learnt to respect Jock too.

By the time he was three months old all the other puppies had gone to their new masters and he and Jess were the only dogs left with the wagons. Then Jock 'went to school'. Like all schoolboys, he learnt the things that he enjoyed very quickly but when he hated something he learnt it very slowly indeed. He was as happy as could be when I poked about with a stick in the bank of a donga to turn out a mouse or a field rat. He enjoyed hunting for a partridge or a hare that I had hidden. But he hated it when I made him lie down and watch my gun or coat while I pretended to go off and leave him. And as for his lessons in manners – well, he detested them!

The first thing that a dog must learn is that he may not steal. At the outspans the 'grub box' is put on the ground with the big three-legged stew-pot beside it, ready for any man to help himself. This means that if there is a dog thief in the camp no food is safe.

Dogs are like people. They learn best when they are young, so when Jock was still a puppy I taught him not to take food before I gave him permission. I held him back from his saucer of porridge, or tapped him sharply on the nose each time he tried to dive into it. This seemed unkind at first, but after a few days he learnt to wait for my signal. He would lie with his nose right against the saucer and tremble with excitement until he heard me say: 'Take it!' I believe he actually watched my lips, he was so quick to obey when the order came.

Jock learnt many lessons from me and he also learnt a good deal from his mother, Jess. She showed him not to poke his nose against a snake to find out what it was, and to watch carefully before he touched anything strange with his paw. He learnt to know by instinct when things were dangerous and that he must never leave the ring of camp fires when there were lions about.

From me he learnt to be obedient, patient and watchful. He learnt to have good manners and never to steal. In time, I taught him everything a hunting dog should know and above all to go everywhere with me and to be my true friend.

One of the lessons that Jock learnt is that it is not safe for a dog to interfere with a sitting hen. He hated fowls because they kept stealing his food and he finished off several before I taught him how to roll them over instead of killing them. On this occasion Jock scented a hen at our outspan place. He could not see her because she had made her nest in the thick bush. I saw him suddenly stand stock still, one ear cocked and his head down. Then he began to walk slowly forward towards the nest. Just as he reached it, the hen darted out, gave him a vicious peck on the nose and flapped over his head, squawking for dear life. She was gone before he could make a grab at her. When he heard our shouts of laughter he did look foolish!

With good feeding and exercise, Jock soon grew into a fine strong dog. One day, as he lay asleep in the bright sunshine, I suddenly realized that his coat had lost its pale, wishy-washy look. Instead, it was shining like polished gold. Now I could picture him as he was going to be and as he did, in fact grow up – a handsome golden brindle with dark wavy lines on his coat and a snow-white 'V' on his broad chest.

Jock's first hunt

Jock's first experience in hunting was on the Crocodile River where there is always good shooting during the rainless winter months. Many of the streams run dry and the smaller animals come down to the river to drink. Knowing this, beasts of prey such as lions, leopards and wild dogs often lie in wait for them among the reeds.

We had camped beside the river so that our oxen could enjoy the good grazing and fresh water. All day long one or other of us would be pottering about in the reeds, gun in hand, hoping to get something for our cooking-pot.

One morning I took Jock out with me, but only to train him as he was still too young to go hunting. Fairly soon we picked up the spoor of a buck in the soft mud. We were following it noiselessly when suddenly a duiker broke out of the reeds and disappeared into the thick bush. Without waiting for a signal from me, Jock dashed after it. The moment I called him back he stopped in his tracks, looking very guilty and disappointed.

Fortunately for him, he did not have to wait long for the hunt to be on and to have my permission to join in. I was sitting under a thorn tree when I heard the sound of a buck cantering through the sand and a short distance away a second duiker stopped abruptly, half facing me. At such close quarters I could not miss it. I raised my rifle and fired. The buck rolled over and, dropping my gun in my haste, I ran to make sure it was dead.

Now, a hunter should never part with his gun but in my excitement I completely forgot mine. As I ran forward the duiker got up, rolled over and then struggled to its feet again. The bullet had broken its shoulder, but without my gun I could not shoot a second time and put it out of its pain.

All the while Jock had been obediently keeping behind me. When I shouted 'After him!' he was away in a flash, chasing the duiker as it stumbled and plunged in a desperate effort to escape. Jock soon caught up

with it. He leapt at its throat, but despite its injury the duiker was too quick for him and made off. Jock was after it immediately, this time springing from behind. He grabbed at its hind leg so that it fell to the ground. It rolled over, gave a sudden twist and was back on its feet. It turned towards Jock and, with its head lowered, thrust so fiercely at him with its spiky black horns that I thought nothing could save my dog. I rushed to his aid, but before I could reach the buck it had made another dash for freedom.

Jock was after it again at once and down they both came, rolling over and over in the dust. The duiker struggled frantically but I ran forward and managed to grab it by the head. I held it down on the ground with my knee on its neck and my knife in my hand, ready to finish it off. Jock, thinking the fight was over, let go his grip. In a second the duiker had doubled up its body and was lashing at me over its head with its sharp little feet. My knife went flying and with a sudden wrench the buck had freed itself and was away.

Jock had been moving round and round all the while, panting and whimpering anxiously. As soon as the duiker broke away again he sprang at its throat. This time it was Jock who was attacked by the wildly lashing feet. With helpless horror I watched as the buck's razor-sharp hoof caught his right shoulder and ripped the flesh down to the hip. I made a grab at those flailing legs but before I could catch hold of them the kicks grew feeble, the buck lay still and I knew that Jock had won.

The sun was hot. We had a long way to walk and the duiker made a heavy load, but at the end of that exciting first hunt none of those things seemed to matter. All I did care about was the cut on Jock's side, but he did not seem to mind it a bit. All the way back to the wagons his little tail wagged and he was just as happy as a dog can be. Perhaps he was proud of the wound that would show as long as he lived as a scar beneath his golden brindled coat – a memento of his first real hunt.

In the heart of the bush

Jock began life by thinking he could do everything, know everything and go everywhere, as most puppies do. But as he grew older he had to learn to mind his own business, as well as to understand it. An intelligent hunting dog with a stout heart soon gets to know what concerns him and what to leave alone. And while he is learning these things he becomes more and more keen on his own work.

And there was no doubt about it, Jock was certainly keen. When I took down my rifle from the wagon he did not begin to bark wildly, as most sporting dogs do. He would look up at me quickly and give a little whimper of joy, make two or three springing bounds and shake himself as though he had just come out of water. Then, with a soft 'woo-woo-woo' of contentment, he would drop into his place at my heels.

Jock was the best of companions and throughout our years together I never tired of watching him. There was always something to learn from him, some-thing to admire, something to be grateful for. Often there was something to laugh about, in the way we laugh at people we love. Usually it was the struggle be-tween Jock's keenness and his sense of duty that made us laugh. He knew that while out hunting his place was behind me, but often he saw or scented game long before I did and hated waiting for my permission to dash after it.

Jock missed nothing for he was always on the watch. He knew immediately if there was any change in my manner. It was impossible for me to stop and listen or even to turn my head without being noticed. When I realized there was game nearby he sensed it instantly. He kept so close to me that he would bump against my heels or run right into my legs if I stopped suddenly. I could not scold him or give him an order in case I scared off the game. Instead, I started using hand signs which he soon learnt to understand.

Sometimes Jock would annoy me by pressing

against me while I was aiming my rifle. I dared not raise my voice to correct him, so I would turn round slowly and give him a stern look. He knew exactly what it meant. Down would go his ears and he would drop his stump of a tail in a feeble kind of way. Then he would open his mouth into a sort of foolish laugh. 'I beg your pardon,' he seemed to say. 'That was an accident. I won't do it again.'

He looked so funny, it was impossible to be angry with him. He was so keen and he meant so well. When he saw me laughing at him he would come up close to me again, cock his tail as high as it would go and wag it a bit faster.

A dog's tail will tell you a great deal. Look at it and you will know exactly how he is feeling. That was certainly the way I knew what Jock was thinking about one day when we were lost in the veld. And what is more, it was Jock's tail that showed us the way back.

Up till then I had never lost my way while out hunt-ing, though this is something that happens to nearly everyone in the Bushveld at some time. Some men have been lost for days until they accidentally stumbled across a track or were found by a search party. Others have died of hunger or thirst. Some have been killed by lions and only a boot or a coat found in the veld told what had happened. And some have disappeared without trace, never to be heard of again.

I did not want any of these things to happen to me, so when I first went out hunting I took great care not to get lost. I noticed what the trees, rocks and koppies looked like. I remembered which side of the road I had turned off and always made sure of the direction I was taking by the position of the sun. But as days passed and I came to no harm I began to think I was a fine fellow and would never be foolish enough to lose my way. And so I became bolder and more careless until in the end I, too, was lost. It was thanks to Jock that I ever got safely back to the wagons.

A most annoying bird. . .

The 'Go away' bird's more common name is the Grey Loerie. It is a fairly large, silvery-grey bird with a stiff backswept crest on the top of its head and a long, straight tail.

As Percy Fitzpatrick says, hunters find the Grey Loerie extremely annoying. It often follows them, flapping clumsily from tree to tree and alarming the game with its noisy, long drawn-out call. It certainly seems to be warning the animals to 'go away'.

Lost in the veld

At about three o'clock one afternoon, Jock and I set off from our outspan, hoping to find some game for our cooking-pot before the evening trek began.

We had not gone far when Jock began sniffing about busily as if to tell me there was game about. Before I had time to look out for it there was a harsh cry of 'Go 'way! Go 'way!' and an ugly, big-beaked bird flapped down onto a nearby tree.

'Go away' birds are said to warn animals when hunters are coming and, sure enough, just then I saw six splendid kudu move out of the bush and disappear quickly among the trees. I picked up a stone and threw it angrily at the 'Go away' bird which flew off, squawking in alarm.

Jock and I followed the kudu's fresh spoor and before long we came upon them standing majestically at the edge of some thick bush. I stopped, but the kudu saw me and simply melted away before I could raise my rifle.

I did not know it then, but the kudu were simply playing with us. Time and again they allowed us to catch up with them, always stopping where they could see us coming but where it was easy to disappear quickly into the bush.

They led us on and on, Jock sniffing away after their spoor and his tail wagging briskly whenever he found it. But at last not even Jock could help, for the kudu seemed to have vanished altogether.

It was nearly five o'clock and we had wandered a long way from our outspan. I had been too excited to

notice any landmarks on the way and had forgotten to watch the sun. All the same, I was sure that Jock and I would easily find our way home.

I climbed a nearby koppie so that I could look out and see how far we had come. Down below us there were two mimosa trees and an ant-heap that I thought we had passed earlier. I did not realize that in the Bushveld there are thousands of these things, all exactly alike, and that Jock and I could zigzag from one to another for hours without getting anywhere.

And that is exactly what we did, until the sun was low in the sky behind us and I knew we would have to hurry to get back to the camp before dark. As we struggled on my eyes were suddenly dazzled by the setting sun, not behind us this time, but directly ahead. Without knowing it, we must have turned full circle. Then I knew that we were lost.

Once more I climbed a koppie and fired three shots into the air, hoping my friends would hear them and come to look for us. The echoes died away and there was no answer. My own heartbeat and Jock's panting breath were the only sounds in the still evening air.

I sat down with my back against a rock and a strange choky feeling in my throat. We would have to wait for the night to pass before going on, even though I knew there might be lions about. Jock lay down beside me. Now and again he would stir his stumpy tail in the dust, just to show that he understood my loneliness.

But suddenly he was on his feet, ears cocked, listening. I thought he had scented some game, but then I noticed his tail. At first it drooped slightly, then it began to wag gently but steadily from side to side. 'He sees something that he knows,' I said to myself. 'And he's pleased!'

I looked out over his head. There, quite close by, were our own oxen peacefully grazing in the deepening shadows. We scrambled down the koppie and within moments were back in camp.

Later, while we were preparing to trek, Jim Makokel', the big Zulu wagon driver, came to me, smiling in a knowing kind of way. 'What were you shooting at, out there on the koppie?' he asked. 'It must have been a bird or a monkey in a tree. Your bullets went high over the wagons.'

I felt sure he knew what had happened and was secretly laughing at us, so I told him sharply to inspan and not to talk so much.

That night I curled up in my blankets with Jock beside me as usual. 'Good old boy!' I said, giving him an extra pat. 'We know all about it, you and I, but we won't tell a soul!' As I dropped off to sleep I felt a few drowsy pats against my leg and knew it was Jock's tail wagging good night.

The impala stampede

After Jock's first fight with the duiker I knew I could trust him to follow a wounded animal and, if possible to bring it down. Often the bush was so thick that I could not catch up with a fleeing buck so I learnt to rely on Jock as he was smaller and faster than I was. On one occasion, when he disappeared while following wounded game, I thought I had lost him for ever. It happened on an unforgettable day just after we had been caught in an impala stampede.

There is no sight more beautiful than a herd of impala on the move. A whole troop may clear a road or donga in a single effortless leap, their graceful red and white bodies curving like a great wave. You stand and watch, lost in wonder, so that you completely forget to shoot. Yet the picture of grace and beauty that remains in your mind is far better than any trophy for the cooking-pot.

This is how I felt after seeing my first herd of impala, but afterwards there followed hours of anxiety when I thought I would never see Jock again.

We had been out hunting all afternoon and had almost given up hope of seeing game when I caught sight of an impala half hidden by a scraggy bush. Jock was beside me, trembling with excitement. He kept darting glances in every direction, showing that he knew there must be more animals nearby.

Suddenly there was rushing and scrambling on all sides and we found ourselves surrounded by hundreds of leaping and plunging impala. The bush seemed to be alive with them, and the dust they kicked up, the pounding of their feet and the sound of their sneezy snorts completely bewildered me. I stood among them, just gazing in wonder.

The herd must have been dozing after their morning feed when we disturbed them. In their wild panic they could not tell what or where the danger was and I expected to be trampled under foot at any moment. I fired three shots and from the thud of a bullet knew I must have hit something, but the wounded buck rushed on with the rest. Jock dashed ahead of me and I followed, but the day was so hot that I soon grew tired and sat down to rest.

Half an hour passed but Jock did not return. I whistled and called but there was no sign of him. Eventually I decided to return to the wagons, hoping that Jock had found his own way back, but none of the men at the camp had seen him.

When Jim Makokel' heard what had happened he borrowed my gun and went off to look for Jock. Three hours later he returned, silent, hot and dusty. Jock was still nowhere to be seen.

It was time for the wagons to leave on the evening trek but without Jock we would not move. Darkness fell and, knowing that there were lions and leopards on the prowl, I was afraid that my dog would never get back to me alive.

But suddenly there was a loud yell from Jim. 'He has come!' he shouted joyfully. 'He has come back! What did I tell you?'

And there was Jock trotting steadily along the road. Jim rushed to greet him and cried out: 'See the blood! He has fought! He has killed! Dog of all dogs! Jock! Jock!' And Jim's song of triumph broke off in a burst of rough tenderness.

But Jock took no notice of Jim's excited shouts. Slowing down his tired trot, he came straight to me, wagged his tail and gave my hand a splashy lick. Then he turned and looked back down the road, his tail moving slowly from side to side. Far away in the bush something lay dead and this was Jock's way of saying he would show me if only I would follow him.

We were all certain that Jock had pulled down the impala and killed it. What a fight that must have been with an animal eight times his size that had such sharp horns and powerful hoofs! But had Jock fought only the impala? Had hyenas and wild dogs followed the trail of blood and had he fought them too? That is something I shall never know for only Jock could tell.

As Jock lay sleeping that night Jim Makokel' sat staring into the glowing coals of his fire. Every now and then he would mutter: 'Ow, Jock!' click his tongue, shake his head and give the deep chuckle that is the Zulu warrior's way of expressing his admiration for something truly wonderful.

The allies

To Jim Makokel' people were divided into three groups. There were Zulu, white men and the rest. He greeted Zulu as equals but he looked down on all the others, especially the Shangaan. These people, so Jim said, could not fight, nor did they know how to handle animals.

Soon after coming to work for me Jim discovered that he and Jock shared the same dislike and he would openly encourage Jock to attack any stranger who came near our wagons, especially if he happened to be a Shangaan.

In those days gangs of mine-workers used to travel along the road to and from the goldfields of the Eastern Transvaal. About 30 or 40 of them would walk along past our wagons in single file, each man carrying a bundle of blankets, clothing and other possessions balanced on his head.

One day, as a little procession of Shangaans came along our road, Jock strolled out in the friendliest manner and sat down in their path. Innocent though Jock looked, the leader of the group did not trust him and shied off the track into the veld, passing by at a

safe distance. The second Shangaan was a little bolder and passed closer to Jock. The third and fourth dared to walk nearer still until eventually they were almost brushing Jock's nose. All this time he never budged, merely turning his head and following each Shangaan with his eyes.

The whole performance was so funny that we all laughed, even the Shangaans themselves. But as the last man walked past there was a muffled bark and without warning Jock sprang up and nipped him from behind. The man let out such a terrified yell that the whole gang jumped with fright and clutched at their toppling bundles. Meanwhile, Jock raced along the footpath, leaping and snapping in what was, to him, an amusing game.

Despite my disapproval Jim found it amusing too. After that, whenever mine-workers passed by, I would hear him say in a hoarse, low voice: 'Jock! Jock! Shangaans! Catch them, Jock!' Jock's head would be up in a moment and unless I stopped him at once, some sort of romp would be sure to follow.

One day, as I was resting in my wagon, I heard Jim call out the familiar words to Jock in a fierce whisper and, sure enough, a long string of mine-workers was appearing over a nearby hill. Straight away Jock trotted out into their path, quite prepared to repeat his old trick of standing in their way, and once again it was the last man who was attacked from behind.

Jim burst into great bellows of laughter, but the Shangaans did not think that the incident was funny. They were on their way home, taking with them new blankets, bright enamel plates and mugs and small painted tin trunks. As Jim continued to roar with laughter I saw one of them draw from his bundle a brand new axe. The bright steel flashed in the sun as he brandished it above his head and strode towards Jock, muttering angrily. With a scrambling bound Jim rushed at the man, his laughter turned to rage. In one hand he held a fighting stick and in the other an assegai. The Shangaan stopped, the axe still held high, but Jim went for him with leaps and blood-curdling yells. The stick came down with a whirr and the Shangaan dropped unconscious.

I had shouted myself hoarse at Jim but he heard nothing. He snatched the axe from the Shangaan's hand and lashed out at the nearest man while Jock, excited by my agitated shouts, joined in the fighting for all he was worth.

It was half an hour before I could calm Jim down. The Shangaans had all disappeared, leaving their precious goods scattered on the ground. Jim wanted to gather them all as loot but I sent him back to his place under the wagon.

Presently a head appeared over the rise, then another and another until, very cautiously, the Shangaans crept back. They quietly collected all their possessions – all, that is, except the axe that caused the trouble, for that was nowhere to be seen. But the next day, while camped at our first outspan, I saw Jim Makokel', not at all ashamed of himself, busily carving his mark on the handle under my very nose!

Jess and the porcupine

During the hot wet summers, when fever made it dangerous to trek across the Bushveld, we camped high up on the edge of the Berg. Here Ted and I worked at cutting timber for the goldfields. Surrounding us were rugged mountain gorges, tumbling waterfalls and kloofs festooned with tree-ferns and creepers.

Jock and Jess were together again after many months apart. Now I could see how alike they were and yet, in some ways, how different. Jess certainly was ugly but she was brave and faithful too. All the good in her handsome son came from her.

The two dogs had some fine sport together near our camp. One day they caught an ant bear. On another they killed a wild cat as big as they were and armed with the fiercest of claws. Often there were races with baboons but we did not encourage them. A dog stands little chance against a full-grown male, even if it is on its own.

One day we were visited by a grizzled old man with a head-ring of polished wax which showed that he was a person of importance in his tribe. He greeted us politely and, with the help of Jim Makokel', told us why he had come.

His kraal had been attacked by a leopard, the biggest ever seen. Dogs, goats, pigs and even fowls had been taken and two days before it had carried off a precious heifer calf in broad daylight. The old man was poor and the leopard had nearly ruined him. He had heard that we were great hunters and now he asked us to come to his kraal and kill the thief.

Next afternoon we set off, taking guns and a leopard trap. By nightfall we had reached the foot of the Berg, struggling along paths you might think only a baboon could follow.

In brightest moonlight we made our way through the thick undergrowth, led on by the shadowy figure of the old man. Suddenly Jock and Jess startled us by barking furiously and rushing into the bush beside the path. Then there was a scuffling noise, followed by grunting, a crash and scramble and the clear yelp of a dog. 'Ingwa! Ingwa!' ('Leopard! Leopard!') shouted the old man. 'He has killed the dogs!'

With guns ready we peered into the darkness, not knowing what to expect. Then we heard a rustle in front and a whimper of pain. Jess came limping towards us through the shadows, shaking her head and rubbing her mouth against her paws. There was no sign of Jock but the grunting sounds still came from the bush. Moving cautiously forward, we parted some thick branches and there, in a moonlit space, was Jock. Standing on his hind legs and using his sharp teeth, he was dragging and tugging at an animal bigger than he was.

With a wild yell, Jim shot past me and plunged his assegai into the struggling creature. 'Porcupine! Porcupine!' he shouted, and we were all round it in sec-

onds. Jock had it by the soft, bare underside of the throat and I think it was as good as dead before Jim's assegai struck it.

We cut up the body as meat, using the unwanted parts to bait the leopard trap which we set under a big tree. With any luck we might find the thief caught there next morning.

Then we settled down for the night beside the camp fire. In the bright light of the flames I could see that Jock's white chest was speckled with blood where he had been pricked by the porcupine's sharp quills. One of them, long and stiff, and as thick as a pencil, had pierced Jess's foot. Ted had managed to pull it out but we still could not understand why she moved restlessly from place to place and kept whimpering and rubbing her muzzle on her paws.

Ted was still worried about her next morning. Taking her head in his hands, he asked: 'What is it, Jess, old girl?' Suddenly he gave a shout of pain for something had pricked his hand. Very gently he examined Jess's head and found that the porcupine had shot a quill clean through her lip and gum so that its sharp tip had emerged just below her ear. Using pliers and a skinning knife, Ted and I eventually pulled it out and found it to be over 15 centimetres long. Poor old Jess! She did struggle and whimper a little as we tugged at the quill, but never once did that brave dog give a cry of pain.

On the edge of the Berg. . .

No landscape in South Africa is more majestically beautiful than the edge of the Berg. This is the escarpment which separates the high plains of the Transvaal from the rolling grasslands of the Bushveld a thousand metres below, and stretches some 300 kilometres from south to north. Racing rivers plummet down spectacular gorges and fling themselves into deep, fern-shaded ravines. Mists swirl round solitary buttresses of stark rock where eagles build their nests, and in the deep wooded kloofs monkeys and bush pigs, baboons, buck and even leopards make their homes.

Until man learned to conquer the dreaded diseases of malaria and ngana, fear of fever kept men out of the Bushveld in the hot, wet summer months. During this season Percy Fitzpatrick and his friends would remain on the high ground at the edge of the Berg and return to transport riding only in the cool autumn, when they were safe from disease.

Leopard and baboons

There was no holding Jess. She seemed none the worse for her wounds and, lively as ever, joined Jock and the rest of us when we set off after the leopard.

Earlier one of the chief's scouts had brought news to the camp. 'That old skelm!' he said. 'He has sprung the trap and run away. By now he will be far away hiding in a krans.'

We hurried to the trap where the leopard's footprints could be plainly seen around the big tree. Some hair and skin had been caught in the teeth of the trap but there was no sign of blood. The leopard must have released the spring as it pounced at the meat but somehow it had managed to get away without being seriously injured.

We looked at one another, disappointed. It would be very difficult to track the leopard without a trail of blood to follow, but we were determined not to give up the hunt.

With the chief's scouts leading us, we followed the bed of a mountain stream that was shaded by tall trees. One of the guides stopped abruptly and without a word pointed with his assegai at the two dogs. They had gone ahead and were both standing still, looking steadily upstream. The hair on their backs and shoulders was bristling and they were growling softly. It was then that we noticed the fresh spoor of the leopard at the water's edge and knew that we were on its trail.

Noses to the ground, the dogs trotted along a tunnel through the undergrowth and up a steep, rocky krans. We had just followed them out into the open when once again they stopped in their tracks. They stood together quivering and bristling all over, noses up, sniffing the air. There was no doubt of it – they had caught the scent of the leopard very close by.

Breathlessly, we waited to see what would happen. Then suddenly there was a snarling roar from the hillside just above us and the leopard shot like a yellow streak from the cave that was its lair. One crashing bound followed another as it sprang across our path and into the bush. Before we had time to raise our rifles it had disappeared and there was silence.

There seemed no point in following the leopard any further. It was thoroughly alerted now and would probably hide in some place which we could not reach.

We decided to move on in the hopes of shooting a wild pig for our dinner.

We had gone only a short distance when a loud 'Waugh!' from a baboon echoed across the ravine. It sounded like a warning cry from a sentry that had seen us. When we looked into the gorge below we saw a troop of baboons stealing quietly into the undergrowth. Before they had time to cross the stream there was a sudden shriek of agony and our blood seemed to freeze in horror. Immediately hundreds of agitated baboons rushed out of the bush and, barking and bellowing, clambered up the rocky hillside. Once they were clear of the trees their mad scramble ceased and they turned and began hurling rocks into the ravine below.

'Look out!' shouted Jim Makokel', pointing towards the bush. 'There is the leopard!'

And there it was, its long, spotted body crouched on a flat rock, its left paw pinning down the struggling body of a captured baboon.

Roaring with rage, the baboons formed a tightly packed semi-circle and surged down the hillside towards the leopard. It darted swift glances at the horde, then its nerve snapped and with one spring it shot away into the bush.

Instantly the baboons rushed forward to rescue their injured comrade. Then the whole troop scrambled up the slope again, two of them taking the arms of the leopard's victim and helping it to safety.

We were still gazing at the baboons with amazement when once more Jim cried out in alarm. 'The dogs!' he shouted. 'Where are the dogs?' I turned cold with fear. If the dogs had followed the maddened mob of baboons they were as good as dead.

Then, to my relief, I caught sight of them moving cautiously along the river bed, noses up, scenting the air. We knew what they were after. With loaded rifles and breath held hard we watched intently. Then, over the edge of a big rock just above the dogs, the leopard appeared. Stealthily it crept forward until it looked down, ready to pounce, at Jock and Jess.

Three rifles cracked, and with a howl the leopard shot over the dogs' heads. It plunged down the stony river bed, rolled over and lay motionless. It had been shot through the heart.

Buffalo and bush fire

My friend Francis, who was a great hunter, believed the buffalo to be the most dangerous animal in the Bushveld. When angry it gives its enemy little chance of escape for it will charge at him and, with a quick and powerful twist of its massive horns, toss him high over its back. I shall never forget the first time Jock and I saw a buffalo, for because of it we were almost swept to our death in a bush fire.

The summer was over and we were back in the Bushveld. Francis had promised to show me a place at the foot of the Berg where we might see some really big game, so one morning we set off with Jock, little knowing what was in store for us.

Quite soon we reached a stream where the muddy banks had been well trodden by animals coming down to drink. As Francis bent down to examine some big footprints he gave a grunt of satisfaction. 'I thought so!' he said. 'Buffalo have been here!'

We followed their spoor which led upstream and then swerved off towards the hills. The buffalo had trampled the long grass into a broad track which led us to the edge of thick bush. Here Jock stopped, head erect, ears cocked and tail poised – dead still. Silently we stared into the shadows, and there we spotted a buffalo calf peacefully standing under a big tree. Suddenly a twig snapped and in an instant we were surrounded by surging and angry buffalo. Afraid that they would charge, Francis raised his rifle and fired.

We heard the bullet thud against something big and then, in a wild stampede of panic, the herd plunged away from us through the bush. Jock was beside me, straining to go after them, but at the sight of my hand raised in a signal to 'stay' he reluctantly lay down.

Any buffalo is dangerous, but a wounded one is to be avoided at all costs. Knowing this, we were doubly cautious as we followed the trail of blood through a deeply wooded ravine. Eventually the gorge widened into a broad valley where we paused, uncertain what to do next for there was no sign of the wounded buffalo.

Then, from a distance, we heard the curious, far-travelling sound of Africans calling to one another. 'They're after the wounded buffalo!' cried Francis. 'Quick, or we'll never see him again!'

Up the rough track we stumbled, but suddenly a cloud of smoke blew into our faces, blinding and choking us. 'They're burning the slopes to drive the buffalo out!' exclaimed Francis angrily. 'Back to the ravine before the flames catch up with us!'

But it was too late, for we had no chance of winning the race against the rushing sea of flames. Our only hope was to burn a patch of ground between us and the fire and in this way stop the fire from spreading. Using bunches of dry grass as torches, we lit a wide stretch of grass and soon flames were leaping into the air like a blazing sheet. When we opened our scorched eyes the ground in front of us was charred and black.

Then, down on the wings of the wind roared the other fire and before it fled every living thing. A herd of kudu came crashing by, followed by wildebeest rushing forward with lowered heads. A reedbuck ram, wild-eyed and terrified, galloped past and a hare, its ears laid back flat, scuttled between Francis and me. A troop of monkeys, shrieking with terror, scampered by while a pair of toktokkie beetles made pathetically slow progress over the scorching sand. Porcupine, ant-bear, meerkat – they were all fleeing. Even a black mamba, most deadly snake of all, came sailing out of the flaming grass with swaying head and glittering eyes.

Francis and I stood on our own burnt patch, shielding ourselves from the awful heat with branches torn from trees. Jock had no protection, so I held him in my arms while myriads of sparks showered down on us, burning holes in our clothing and blistering our skin.

Then, just when the flames were fiercest, there came a sudden gasp and sob and the fire died behind us as it reached the bare black ground. Our patch had acted as a firebreak and the blaze could get no farther.

Faint from heat and exhaustion, we reached camp long after dark. Jock had suffered too, for his paws were so badly burnt that he could not put them to the ground. As for the wounded buffalo – we had forgotten all about him. He seemed part of another life!

Jock and the wild dogs

One winter evening we were gathered as usual round the camp fire when Jock, who was dozing at my feet, suddenly raised his head, growled and stiffened. Then he got up and trotted briskly to the edge of the camp site. He stood there, staring intently into the darkness, his ears cocked and listening.

We watched and waited, and then in the distance we heard the mournful howl of a wild dog. There was silence for a moment and the cry was answered, but closer to us this time. A third call followed, then another and another until the night air echoed with eerie sounds, each one seeming to come from a different direction.

'Ai!' exclaimed Jim Makokel'. 'The wild dogs are hunting. They are calling to tell each other where they are and where to find the buck they are chasing.'

Wild dogs, so Jim told us, always hunt in the same way. First they choose their prey, usually a ewe with a young calf, and drive it away from the rest of the herd. But the wild dogs know that buck are much faster than they are, so these clever animals hunt their prey in relays. The first pair drops out when it is tired and a second pair takes over, and when the second pair tires a third pair is ready to fall in. So the wild dogs keep up the chase, never allowing the buck a moment's rest. Eventually it drops, exhausted, and the whole pack goes in for the kill. What a cruel method of hunting it seemed!

As Jim talked, Jock was moving round and round in the bright circle of the camp fire, always keeping on the side closest to the baying voices of the dogs. Suddenly the scattered howls ceased and for a moment all was quiet. Then, coming from only one direction and drawing steadily closer to the camp, we heard the excited cries of the entire pack.

Jock was trembling, but I motioned him to my side

and without a word we all took up our guns. Then with a wild cry, like the sound of a coming flood, the hunt was upon us and into our circle of light there burst a terrified impala ewe. With open mouth, despairing eyes and ears spread wide, she plunged forward in a last staggering lurch and tumbled exhausted at our feet.

After her raced the leader of the pack, intent upon the kill. Another dog followed, then another and another, but they all dropped under a volley of bullets and flying assegais. Still the pack rushed on until, warned by the check in front, the dogs stopped at the edge of the clearing. We could not see their shadowy shapes distinctly, but over 20 pairs of eyes, glowing in the firelight, shone at us from the darkness.

Jock could be held back no longer. He shot towards the pack like a rocket, grabbing the nearest dog by the throat. I shouted, but before he could hear my warning cries a second dog was on him.

He let go his grip on the first dog, caught the other one by the ear and flung it to the ground. Then he returned to attack the wounded dog. Jock moved with the skill of a gymnast but I managed to catch hold of him and dragged him out of the way while my companions fired shots at the two wild dogs. They fell dead, and instantly the row of lights at the edge of the clearing went out. There was a rustle and the sound of padded feet and the dim grey forms faded away into the bush.

Meanwhile the impala, dazed and helpless, stood beside us on unsteady, widespread legs. Her breath came in dry, choking sobs and the look of wild terror was still in her eyes. We offered her a bowl of water and she drank greedily and then lay down, still struggling to regain her breath.

For half an hour she remained on the ground, slowly recovering. Then she rose to her feet, looked carefully about her and proudly and deliberately walked away.

At the fringe of the bush the ewe stopped and turned her head, giving us one last, long look. 'Goodbye,' she seemed to say, 'and thank you!' And with a flick of her sensitive ears and a whisk of white tail, the beautiful gentle creature slipped safely into the dark.

25

Jock's mistake

Halfway between the Crocodile and Komati rivers there is one of the most delightful spots in the Bushveld. Broad grasslands stretch between scattered koppies and even though there is no running water there in winter, there are several big pools with shady trees around them. Game is plentiful and it was here that I saw my first big mixed herd. And, on the following day, it was here that Jock made his terrible mistake.

I came across the place while out hunting with Jock and my old pony, Snowball. We had a large camp of wagons and, as we needed meat for the men, I set off early to see what I could find. For some hours there was no sign of game so at about midday I tethered Snowball in a patch of good grass while I rested in the shade with Jock snoozing beside me.

After a while he got up, sniffed the air and began to walk upwind. Feeling sure he must have scented something, I decided to follow him. We had not gone far when we came across a herd of about a hundred impala and, just behind them, a fair-sized group of tessebe. It was a beautiful sight. The animals were not feeding or resting but simply moving about, relaxed and unconcerned.

I was watching them with admiration when Jock's attention was attracted to something a little to our right. It was a herd of blue wildebeest and with them were about a dozen quagga. They were all exactly alike and stood staring at me, forefeet neatly together, ears pricked and their heads quite still.

Something must have disturbed the impala for suddenly the whole herd swept off, leaping and curving like one animal. At this the tessebe took fright and galloped off, the quagga thundered away like a stampede of horses and the wildebeest simply vanished.

On the way back to the wagons I managed to bring down a fine big reedbuck ram for the men's dinner. If there was any meat over we would dry it to make biltong for the days to come when we would have no fresh meat.

Hoping for another glimpse of the mixed herd, I returned to that pleasant spot early the next morning. Not for a moment did I dream that one of the worst of days was in store for Jock and me.

All went well until we unexpectedly came across a herd of grazing kudu. They cantered away when they saw us but I fired a shot as they turned. A big cow at the end of the troop stumbled and Jock was after her in a flash. He must have thought that she had been hit and that there was a broken leg to grip, but he was mistaken. He made a dive at her from behind but the cow was uninjured and lashed out at him viciously. Her foot struck Jock under the jaw with such force that he flew into the air in a backward somersault.

'Jock!' I shouted in horror. I ran to where he lay motionless on the ground, the blood oozing from his mouth, nose and eyes. There was no sign of breath or heartbeat so I ran to the pool nearby and filled my hat with water. I poured it over Jock and into his mouth but still he did not move. Back I went to the pool and when I was returning with a second supply of water my heart gave a great jump. There was Jock, sitting up under the thorn tree and wagging his groggy head, his eyes dazed and blinking.

'Good boy!' I exclaimed joyfully. 'Good old Jock!' He took no notice at all, but at the touch of my hand his ears pricked up and his stumpy tail scraped feebly in the dead leaves. He lapped a little water and with a great effort stood up. Then he lurched into a staggering run, looking 'fight' all over. There was no doubt about it, Jock was after the kudu cow.

I shouted at him, ordering him to stop but he paid no heed. Then I ran after him to bring him back. The moment he saw me he stopped, obeying my signal with a limp air of disappointment.

And from that day on Jock was to depend entirely on signs instead of spoken orders. His disobedience had not been deliberate. It was simply that he could not hear my voice. The blow on the head from the kudu's powerful kick had left Jock stone deaf – as long as he lived he was never to hear another sound.

The quagga

Percy Fitzpatrick must have been one of the last people to see a live quagga. Once this small, zebra-like animal was found ranging the drier parts of South Africa in large herds but today it no longer exists. During the second half of the nineteenth century its unusual striped skin was so much in demand that it was hunted down until not a single quagga remained alive. A stuffed and mounted specimen of a quagga may be seen in the South African Museum in Cape Town.

The old crocodile

We reached the Crocodile River one Sunday morning after a very dry and dusty night's trek. The first thing I did was to go down to the river for a good wash in a clear pool, keeping a sharp lookout all the time for crocodiles.

Breakfast was ready when I returned to the wagons and, dressed in clean clothes, I had hardly sat down when a herd boy arrived from a nearby kraal. As Jim Makokel' listened to what the boy had to say, a look of growing alarm spread over his face. Then, grabbing his sticks and assegais, he called out to me: 'Big crocodile! Groot krokodil! Come and catch him!'

It seemed that the biggest crocodile ever seen in those parts was terrorizing the whole neighbourhood. Within the last year it had taken four men who had been on their way to the goldfields, and a woman and her baby. Many dogs, goats and calves had also disappeared from the drinking place. Seeing our wagons arrive, the people had sent a messenger to beg us for help.

Jim, Jock and I made straight for the pool where I had bathed a short time before and there, basking on a spit of sand in mid-stream, lay a huge crocodile. I raised my gun to aim at it, but the old villain must have seen the metal barrel glinting in the sunlight. Without making a splash he slipped into the water and disappeared.

Angry and disappointed, Jim and I turned to go, but just then there was a call from the opposite side of the river. 'They say he is coming up on another sand-bank,' said Jim. We looked upstream and as we watched, something that looked like a long grey rock rose slowly to the surface. It was the old crocodile.

Meanwhile, a large crowd of people from the kraal had gathered on the river bank and were waiting for me to shoot. Wasting no time, I fired and heard the bullet thump as it buried itself in the crocodile's body. The great beast gave a roar of fury and hurled itself backwards into the water, churning it up into a foaming turmoil. Instantly, there were wild shouts and yells and the men on the bank rushed down to the water's edge with their assegais, eager to finish off their enemy.

The crocodile had disappeared with its first plunge, but moments later it rose again a little nearer to where we stood. Jim dashed into the water, assegai in hand, and I followed, holding my rifle above my head.

In all the confusion I had completely forgotten about Jock, but then I heard a whimpering yelp of excitement and turned to see him spring into the river and swim strongly towards the crocodile. I shouted to stop him, but of course he was deaf to my cries and paddled on, his eyes gleaming with excitement. As soon as he reached the crocodile, Jock made a dive for it and just then the men on the bank let fly with their assegais. Lifting my rifle clear of the water, I fired another shot. The enraged crocodile, wounded by both bullet and assegai, turned towards Jock, its huge jaws wide open. For one horrified moment I watched, sick and helpless, but just as the crocodile reached Jock, it sank again into the water. Once more it rose, this time just beyond the dog and, with a furious lash of its tail, hurled him into the air. Jock hit the water with a splash and as he came to the surface he merely shook the water from his head and returned to the attack.

I knew that unless I came to his rescue Jock would soon be killed by the furious crocodile. Somehow I struggled through water up to my chest and clambered on to a rock. I raised my rifle, but luck was against me. My foot slipped on the wet surface and, gun and all, I tumbled into the muddy river. Quickly I scrambled back onto the rock and was just in time to see the crocodile give one final heave and roll over, dead.

While I waded into the river to retrieve my rifle, Jim and his friends, shouting and laughing in triumph, hauled the crocodile's heavy body to the bank. With Jock swimming behind and making frantic and futile attempts to grab its tail in his teeth, and my hat bobbing along in front, they made a lively procession. My Sunday change of clothes was wasted – but what did that matter so long as we got the old crocodile in the end?

Insects that killed

A hundred years ago the Bushveld was a place to be avoided during the hot, wet summer months, for then the danger of fever was greatest. Conditions were ideal for tsetse fly, carrier of sleeping-sickness to man and the dreaded ngana to cattle. It breeds in warm, damp, shady places such as those found in the Bushveld along the river banks. Fortunately, wild animals do not suffer from ngana but it was this disease that brought death to Percy Fitzpatrick's oxen.

Another dreaded form of fever common in the Bushveld was malaria. The anopheline mosquito, which carries this disease, lays its eggs in exposed pools of water which form after summer rain has fallen. It was not until some years after Percy Fitzpatrick had left the Bushveld that Sir Ronald Ross, an English bacteriologist, discovered that this particular mosquito was responsible for spreading malaria. Only then were scientists able to combat this disease successfully.

His duty

Our last trek was over. First there had been drought, the worst anyone could remember. Then floods had followed and destroyed my wagons. Worst of all, fever swept through the Bushveld and every one of my oxen died. I had no choice but to give up the transport business and find work in the town.

Jim Makokel', the big Zulu wagon driver who had seen it all through with never a grumble, went home to his kraal and his wives. I watched him wave from the wagon that took him away, and the last thing I heard was an uproarious shout of goodbye to Jock. And Jock seemed to know that it was a special occasion, for he stood beside me looking down the road with his ears cocked, his head tilted sideways and his little tail stirring gently.

And so I moved to Barberton. All that was left of the old life was Jock, and soon there was no place in the new life even for him. Out in the veld his deafness did not seem to matter, but in the busy town I was always afraid he would be run over by a wagon or trampled to death by a horse or an ox. At first he was very watchful but soon he became careless and on several occasions he narrowly missed being run over or trodden on.

One day my old friend Ted passed our way in his wagons and very reluctantly I decided to hand Jock over to his care. It would only be a matter of time, I thought, until I had a better and a safer home for him. Meanwhile, he would have something of the old life, trekking and hunting with Ted as he used to do with me.

I heard of him often after that for many people knew Jock and were glad to bring me news. Then Ted had to go to Scotland for a few months and he left Jock with our friend Tom Barnett who kept a trading store. I was not happy about Jock acting watchdog though I told myself that for a short time it would not matter. Tom was always having trouble with thieves and scavenging dogs from the nearby kraals, and there was no knowing what Jock might do with thieves, whether human or dog. He was a hunting dog and when he fought it was to kill.

Tom's chief worry was with his fowls. Night after night kraal dogs broke through the reed fence surrounding the fowl-run and killed the chickens. Jock was deaf to the squawking but it would wake Tom and he would seize his gun and rush outside. Usually he was too late and arrived in the fowl-run to find the damage done and the thieves escaped. But if he had time to wake Jock the scavengers did not stand a chance, for he was quicker than they were.

Often I wondered whether Jock would ever be able to settle down to a life of ease and idleness with me in the town. Would it not be better, I asked myself, for him to die in the veld in a moment of victory than to fade slowly away, to lose his strength and fire and no longer be himself?

Well, Jock is dead now and lies buried under the big fig tree near Tom Barnett's store, and this is how it happened.

One bright moonlit night Tom was once again awakened by the squawking of his fowls. He jumped out of bed and stood at the window, his gun resting on the sill, waiting for the thief. The noise of the fowls died down and, listening carefully, Tom could hear a gurgling and scratching in the fowl-house. It seemed that the scavenger was enjoying his meal there.

'Go on! Finish it!' muttered Tom grimly. 'I'll get you if I have to wait till morning.'

So he stood at the window, patiently watching. And at last the dim form of a dog appeared from the fowl-house and stood for a moment in the deep shadow of the little porch. Tom lifted his gun and took careful aim. The sound died away and the smoke cleared. Stretched out on the ground lay the still figure of the dog. Tom went to bed, satisfied.

The morning sun shone in Tom's eyes as he opened the gate in the reed fence and made his way to the fowl-house. Under the porch, where the sunlight touched it, something shone like burnished gold.

Jock was stretched out on his side – it might have been in sleep. But on his snow-white chest there was a single red spot. And inside the fowl-house lay the kraal dog – dead.

Jock had done his duty.

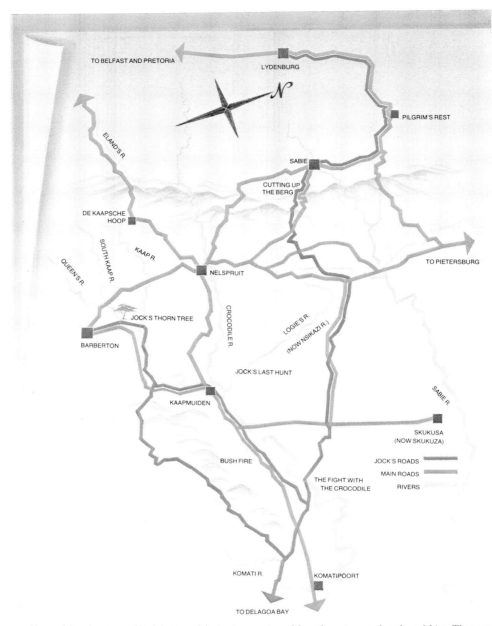

Many of the adventures of Jock happened during journeys to and from the east coast of southern Africa. The route followed by the transport riders of the time, including Sir Percy Fitzpatrick, would have taken them through the southern parts of what is today South Africa's premier game reserve, the Kruger National Park, which was proclaimed in 1926. The Park is proud of its link with Jock, and commemorating him is the 'Jock of the Bushveld' memorial about 18 kilometres north of the Malelane Gate. Jock is close to the hearts of the people of the Lowveld and there are many other places which honour his memory including a statue in the Barberton Park and a large acacia tree outside the town where dog and master often camped. There is even a 'Jock of the Bushveld Trail' which is run by the Wilderness Leadership School in the Hans Hoheisen Private Game Reserve.

Struik Publishers (Pty) Ltd
(a member of Struik New Holland Publishing (Pty) Ltd)
Cornelis Struik House
80 McKenzie Street
Cape Town 8001

Reg. No.: 54/00965/07

First published in hardcover 1986
Second impression 1987
First edition in softcover 1991
10 9 8 7 6

Designer Angus McBride
Cover Designer Robert Meas
Illustrator Angus McBride

Reproduction by Syreline, Cape Town
Printed and bound by Kyodo
Printing Co (Singapore) Pte Ltd

ISBN 0 86978 477 3

56TH FIGHTER GROUP

By Larry Davis

DON GREER

squadron/signal publications